CHARLIE Hits It Big

By Deborah Blumenthal

Illustrated by Denise Brunkus

SCHOLASTIC INC.
New York Toronto London Auckland Sydney
Mexico City New Delhi Hong Kong Buenos Aires

To Sophie, who said, "Ma, why don't you write a book about Charlie?"
And to Charlie, the world's sweetest guinea pig
—D. Blumenthal

For Deirdre, my Big City friend
—D. Brunkus

ISBN-13: 978-0-545-15557-1
ISBN-10: 0-545-15557-6

Text copyright © 2007 by Deborah Blumenthal.
Illustrations copyright © 2007 by Denise Brunkus. All rights reserved.
Published by Scholastic Inc., 557 Broadway, New York, NY 10012,
by arrangement with HarperCollins Children's Books, a division of
HarperCollins Publishers. SCHOLASTIC and associated logos
are trademarks and/or registered trademarks of Scholastic Inc.

12 11 10 9 8 7 6 5 4 3 2 1   9 10 11 12 13 14/0

Printed in the U.S.A.   40

First Scholastic printing, February 2009

Typography by Jeanne L. Hogle

When Sophie woke up and went to feed her guinea pig, she was in for a surprise.

Charlie wasn't there.

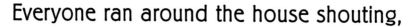
Everyone ran around the house shouting,

"Charlie, Charlie,

Nothing. Not a squeal.
Not a squeak. Nothing but a note.

The family looked at one another. "The coast?"

Then Annie looked into Charlie's cage.

"A CLUE!" Annie shouted.

Meanwhile, high up in the clouds, a 747 was preparing to descend to Los Angeles, California. On board, munching a vegetarian lunch, was Charlie.

"Will there be anything else?" the flight attendant asked him.

"Got any carrot juice?"

"Tomato," the flight attendant said.

"Tomato then," Charlie said. "On the rocks, baby."

At the airport, Charlie got into a taxi.

"Where to?"

"HollyWOOD,"

Charlie said, rubbing his paws together.

After checking into a hotel, Charlie boarded a tour bus.

But when they got to a movie studio, Charlie crept away
from the group and followed a sign that said CASTING.

After waiting on a long line, Charlie was given a paper with words to read.

For the part in the movie, Charlie had to pretend that he was a man with a broken heart.

With his eyes filled with tears, Charlie stared at the camera. Dropping to his knees and pounding his paw against his heart, he cried,

"Find room in your heart to love a beast like me again, and I'll make you the happiest woman alive."

"Cut!" said a man wearing a beret. "Come back tomorrow," he said. "But lose the tan fur—we're looking for dark and handsome."

"No problema," Charlie said.

The next day, a dark and handsome Charlie came back.
With a beautiful actress by his side, he said his line again.

"Find room in your heart to love a beast like me again, and I'll make you the happiest woman alive!"

"Cut!" shouted the director. "You got the part!
You're going to be BIG," he said.

"*BIG!*"

On the way back to the hotel, Charlie
bought a postcard to send home.

Dear Sophie,
Look for me
on the BIG
screen!
What a life!
Charlie

To:
Sophie
at
Home

That night the director was going to have a party for him.
Charlie needed something special to wear.
He walked into a fancy shop.

"Can we help you, sir?"
"Indeed," Charlie said.

Minutes later Charlie emerged from the dressing room.
He admired himself in the mirror and strutted around in
his fine new outfit.

Now it was party time. There was a long buffet table with all kinds of good things to eat.

This was the moment he'd been waiting for. Charlie's mouth was watering.

Fruity-Nut Buffet.
Where was the Fruity-Nut Buffet?
It had to be there—it was a party for *him*.

Charlie searched the table.

Nothing.

Not a sesame seed.

Not a pumpkin seed.

Not even a speck of dried fruit.
He settled for salad.

Then he met lots of people.
"Darling," people called him.
"Mon amour."

They hugged him, winked at him, blew kisses in the air,
and pumped his paw up and down, up and down.
But Charlie didn't even know them.
He didn't know what to say.

Photographers snapped his picture over and over until he saw spots in front of his eyes.

The room got so crowded that people were crushing him and stepping on his little feet.

Charlie felt as if he couldn't breathe!

Everyone loved him. He had new clothes and a tummy full of salad, and he was a Big Pig in HollyWOOD. So why did he feel afraid and lonelier than ever?

He dropped to the floor and crawled to the door.

He thought about Sophie and how they used to play together.

He thought about how he used to sit on her lap while she fed him baby carrots and scratched his neck until he fell asleep.

He thought about being home again, in Sophie's room, without any pushy people.

And how could he *not* think of the Pet Food Emporium opening in their town with ads that said:
Fruity-Nut Buffet
Buy 1, Get 1 Free!

Charlie leaped up and ran back to his hotel. He packed up all his clothes,

went into the fancy bathroom, and took the almond soap, coconut shampoo, and shoeshine cloth.

Then he went to the lobby.

"Taxi," he said, waving a paw.

Hours later, he was back in his small hometown.
When he got to his front door, he knocked and knocked.
No one answered.

Finally, a light went on.
"Who is it?" said a voice from behind the door.
"It's me," said Charlie.

The door opened a crack. Sophie stared and stared.
"Charlie, is that you?" she asked. But before he could
answer, Sophie scooped up Charlie in her arms and
squeezed him.

"Charlie, Charlie," Sophie said.

"You came back!"

"Yes," Charlie said, dropping his head on Sophie's
soft shoulder.

Charlie looked into Sophie's blue eyes, and then he looked at his cage.

Leaning against it was a big sack of Fruity-Nut Buffet with a red ribbon tied around it.

Charlie smiled a big toothy grin.

"Find room in your heart to love a beast like me **again,** and I'll make you the happiest woman alive!"

"What?" Sophie said, looking at Charlie strangely.

"That's Hollywood talk,"

Charlie said.

"Forget about it."